To everyone who likes the ballet - A.G.

For Mum and Dad - S.McN.

The Sleeping Beauty Ballet invites Tilly The Royal Theatre Saturday 15th June

ORCHARD BOOKS

338 Euston Road, London, NW1 3BH

Orchard Books Australia

Level 17/207 Kent Street, Sydney, NSW 2000

First published in 2007 by Orchard Books

First published in paperback in 2007

ISBN 978 1 84616 619 8

Text © Adèle Geras 2007

Illustrations © Shelagh McNicholas 2007

3 5 7 9 10 8 6 4 2

Printed in China

Orchard Books is a division of Hachette Children's Books, an Hachette UK company.

www.hachette.co.uk

Little Ballet Star

Written by Adèle Geras

Illustrated by Shelagh McNicholas

ORCHARD BOOKS

The Sleeping

I'm so excited, I could burst! Today is my birthday and
I'm going to the theatre to see a ballet from the fairy tale
The Sleeping Beauty. My Auntie Gina is a ballerina and
she's taking me backstage before the show as a special treat.

Backstage, some of the dancers are practising their steps.
"If you put on your ballet shoes, you can join in,"
says Auntie Gina.
I love my ballet shoes. They make my feet feel sparkly.

I do my pliés,

and my very best
'good toes, naughty toes'.

I twirl and spin. Everyone claps!

Auntie Gina takes me to the dressing room.
Three pretty ballerinas are putting on make-up.

One of them strokes some blusher on to my cheeks.
I look like a pink apple!

Then we go up to the wardrobe department,
where the costumes are kept.

"Happy birthday, Tilly," says Margie, the wardrobe mistress. "Would you like to try this on?"
"Ooh, lovely!" I say. "Yes, please!"

She helps me into
a fairy costume,

and I twirl in front
of the mirror.

Next, we go downstairs.

"These are the wings where the dancers wait
until it's time to go on stage," says Auntie Gina.

I tip-tip-tiptoe in my pink shoes.

The stage is *so* big and the lights are dazzle-bright!
They make me blink and feel hot. The scenery is a huge
beautiful painting of Sleeping Beauty's fairytale palace.
It looks almost real.

I can hear music coming from behind the curtains.
I peep at the orchestra tuning their instruments,
making funny noises before they play the
proper music.

The rows of seats are filling up with people,
and I can see Mum!
Auntie Gina says, "The ballet is about to start, Tilly.
You can sit with your mum to watch the show."

Mum asks me if I've had a lovely time and I start to tell her about it, but then the lights go out . . .

I'm so excited, I can hardly breathe. Music fills the whole theatre and it feels like something magical is about to happen . . .

Then the fairies run on to the stage! They're wearing their pretty tutus. And there's Auntie Gina!

Auntie Gina is the most important ballerina of all – she's Sleeping Beauty! Her headdress has pale lilac roses on it, and her tutu glitters and sparkles.
The music makes me want to dance too!

Everyone claps when the ballet is finished, but I clap the loudest. I wish I could see it all over again.

Then Auntie Gina steps through the closed curtains and comes to the front of the stage.

"We have a birthday girl in the audience today," she says, "and it just so happens that she's a little ballerina. Come up here, Tilly, darling!"

I'm going up there!
Up on stage!

The curtains open again and Auntie Gina says,
"Let's do a special birthday dance together."

I've got butterflies in my tummy!

Then the music starts
and I'm dancing,

and twirling,

and flitting,

and floating.

I want to shout,
"I'm dancing on a real stage.
I'm dancing like a real ballerina!"

Then the orchestra plays 'Happy Birthday' and I do my very best curtsey ever.

Everyone claps and claps.
I'm so happy, I could jump!

Auntie Gina gives me her headdress.
"A birthday present for you, Tilly,"
she says. "You're a wonderful ballerina."

I give her a big hug and say, "Thank you, Auntie Gina."

The Sleeping

Dad's waiting for Mum and me outside the theatre.
He picks me up and carries me all the way to the car.

Beauty

STAGE DOOR

"I'm very tired," I say, as I close my eyes.

"You're our very own Sleeping Beauty," says Dad.

I'm going to dream of the ballet tonight – I just know I am.